Bad Bears and Good Bears

Retold by Rose Impey

Illustrated by *Priscilla Lamont*

ORCHARD BOOKS

Other titles in this series:

Bad Boys and Naughty Girls

Greedy Guts and Belly Busters

Hairy Toes and Scary Bones

I Spy, Pancakes and Pies

If Wishes were Fishes

Knock, Knock! Who's There?

Over the Stile and into the Sack

Runaway Cakes and Skipalong Pots

Silly Sons and Dozy Daughters

Sneaky Deals and Tricky Tricks

Ugly Dogs and Slimy Frogs

ORCHARD BOOKS
96 Leonard Street, London EC2A 4XD
Orchard Books Australia
14 Mars Road, Lane Cove, NSW 2066
First published in Great Britain in 2000
First paperback publication 2000
Text © Rose Impey 2000
Illustrations © Priscilla Lamont 2000
The rights of Rose Impey to be identified as the author
and Priscilla Lamont as the illustrator of this work
have been asserted by them in accordance with the
Copyright, Designs and Patents Act, 1988.
A CIP catalogue record for this book is available
from the British Library.
ISBN 1 86039 971 1 (hardback)
ISBN 1 86039 972 X (paperback)
1 3 5 7 9 10 8 6 4 2 (hardback)
1 3 5 7 9 10 8 6 4 2 (paperback)
Printed in Great Britain

★ CONTENTS ★

Foxy-Fox and the Three Bears

Once upon a time there were
three bears: a great big bear, a
middle-sized bear and a small wee
bear. And in the same wood lived
a young rascal called Foxy-Fox.

One day the three bears went
out for a walk and while they
were out along came Foxy-Fox.

He sneaked up to the house without a sound and opened the door.

First he put
in his sharp
little nose,

then he put in his
sharp little eyes.

Then he put
in his first paw,

then his
second paw,
then another
and another
until he was
right inside.

Then he
look-look-
looked with
his sharp little
eyes to see
what he
could see.

He saw three chairs around a
table: a great big chair, a middle-
sized chair and a small wee chair.

Foxy-Fox thought he would
sit down and have a rest. So first
he sat on the great big chair, but
it was too hard and he slipped
right off.

Then he sat on
the middle-sized
chair, but
it was too
soft and he
sank right in.

Then he sat
on the small
wee chair and
that was just
right, so he
settled into it
for a rest.

But the small wee chair broke
in two and that rascal fell down
with a BUMP!

When he picked himself up
Foxy-Fox sniff-sniff-sniffed with
his sharp little nose to see what
else he could find.

He found three bowls of cream
on the table: a great big bowl,
a middle-sized bowl and a small
wee bowl.

Of all things, Foxy-Fox liked
cream the best. So first he drank
from the great big
bowl but – *ugh!* –
it was too sour.

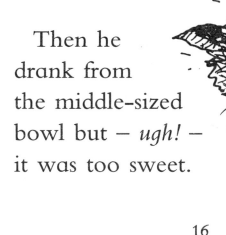

Then he
drank from
the middle-sized
bowl but – *ugh!* –
it was too sweet.

Then he drank from the small wee bowl and – *mmm!* – that was just right! So he drank and drank until it was all gone.

Then that rascal of a fox
climb-climb-climbed up the
stairs, looking for more trouble.

Upstairs he found three beds: a great big bed, a middle-sized bed and a small wee bed.

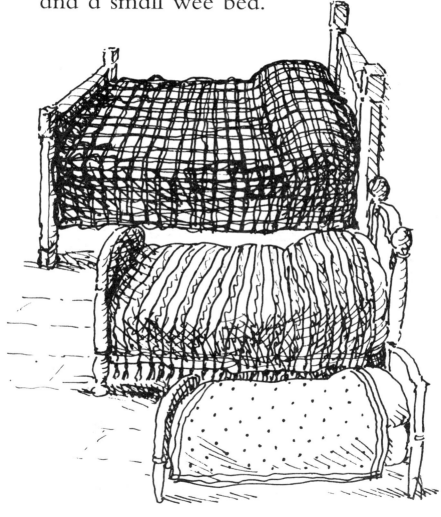

First, he climbed into the great
big bed, but that was hard and
bumpy.

Then, he climbed into the
middle-sized bed, but that was
soft and lumpy.

Then,
he climbed into
the small wee bed and that
was cosy and comfy, so he
rolled over and fell fast asleep.

After a while the three bears
came home. The great big bear
saw his chair and knew at once
someone had been sitting in it.

"Who's been sitting in my
chair?" he said in his great
big voice.

"Who's been sitting in my chair?" said the middle-sized bear in his middle-sized voice.

"Who's been sitting in my chair," said the small wee bear in his small wee voice, "and broken it in two?"

Then the three bears looked
at the table and saw their bowls
of cream.

"Who's been drinking my
cream?" said the great big bear
in his great big voice.

"Who's been drinking my cream?" said the middle-sized bear in his middle-sized voice.

"Who's been drinking my cream," said the small wee bear in his small wee voice, "and drunk it all up?"

Now the three bears were in a temper. They went *stamp-stamp-stamping* up the stairs and into the bedroom.

"Who's been
sleeping in my
bed?" said the
great big bear
in his great
big voice.

"Who's been
sleeping in my
bed?" said the
middle-sized
bear in his
middle-sized voice.

"Who's been sleeping in my bed?" said the small wee bear in his small wee voice. "And look! Here he is!"

Just then, Foxy-Fox woke up
and saw the three bears standing
over him, trying to decide what to
do with him.

"Let's tie him to a tree," said the great big bear in his great big voice.

"Let's put him in a sack and drop him in the river," said the middle-sized bear in his middle-sized voice.

"Let's throw him out of the window," said the small wee bear in his small wee voice.

So that's what they did. The
great big bear took hold of his
front legs, the middle-sized bear
took hold of his back legs, and
the small wee bear shouted,
"One, two, three..."

Foxy-Fox landed with a BUFF!
and a BUMP! and a BANG!

He thought
he must have
broken every
bone in his
body, but he
got up and shook
one leg and that
wasn't broken,

then he shook a
second leg and
that wasn't broken

and then another
and another.

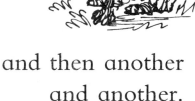

Then he wagged his tail and
that was fine too. So off he ran
home on his fast little feet and
never bothered the bears again.

He ran! He ran!
As fast as he could,
Back to his house
in the deep, dark wood.

The Clever Little Girl and the Bear

One day a little girl went into the
woods to pick berries. But she
wandered too far and got lost.
She called and called, but
no one heard her.

At last she came to a cottage.
She knocked on the door and
when no one answered, she
opened it and went inside.

Now, this was the house of a big brown bear and when he came home and found the little girl he was *delighted*.

"Ho, ho, ho. A little servant to wait on me," he growled. "First you can feed the stove, then you can make me some tea, then you can sweep the floor and tidy my house."

Well, what could the little girl say? You can't argue with a big brown bear.

The poor little girl worked hard every day cooking and cleaning. But all the time she was thinking how to escape. And one day she had an idea.

First she cooked the bear a big plateful of buns to put him in a good mood.

Then she said, "Please, Mr Bear, could I take some buns to my parents?"

"Certainly not," growled the big brown bear.

He wasn't in *that* good a mood. "But then they'll know I'm safe and well," she said.

Hmmm, the big brown bear thought for a moment. "You make the buns," he said, "and I'll take them for you."

This was just what the little girl had hoped he would say.

The very next day she made
another huge plateful of buns.
She put the plate on top of a
very big basket.

"Now, remember," she told the bear. "These buns are for my parents. You mustn't eat any of them. If you do I'll know because I shall be watching you from the roof and I have very good eyesight."

"Yes, yes," growled the big brown bear. "But first I need a little nap."

As soon as the bear was asleep the clever little girl lifted up the plate of buns and climbed into the basket.

When the big brown bear woke,
he lifted the basket onto his back
and set off.

But it was a warm day and the basket was heavy, so he stopped for a rest. He smelled the buns and his mouth began to water. *Mmmm. Mmmm.*

As soon as he reached out for one, a voice said,

Don't touch those buns.
Don't you dare!
I've got my eye on you.
I can see you, Mr Bear.

The big brown bear was surprised. He looked back to his house to see if the little girl was watching him.

"That girl must have good eyesight," he grumbled to himself, "to see such a long way." He jumped up and went on, a bit quicker this time.

But it wasn't long before the bear felt tired again. So he sat down for another rest. Again he looked at the buns.

Just as he reached out for one, a little voice said,

I've told you once,
You'd better take care!
I've got my eye on you.
I can see you, Mr Bear.

This time the big brown bear was frightened. He said to himself, "That girl must have *very* good eyesight to see *such* a long way."

He hurried on and this time he didn't dare stop until he reached the little girl's house.

He knocked on the door.

"Open up! Open up!" he growled. "There's a present here for you."

But the dogs had smelt the bear and they came running from all over the village, snapping and snarling at him.

The bear dropped the basket and ran off, back into the woods, with all the dogs chasing after him.

So when the little girl's parents opened the door they were surprised to see no one there. Just a big basket full of buns.

When they took it inside they were even more surprised. The basket wasn't full of buns, it was full of the clever little girl. She jumped out and threw her arms around them.

Weren't they pleased to have her back! And wasn't she lucky to be back! You can be sure that little girl never went wandering into the woods again. She was far too clever for that.

A tisket! A tasket!
Who's in the basket?
"I am!" said the little girl.

I am!

Sometimes in stories bears are good, kind characters who never do anyone any harm. Sometimes they can be bad and rather scary, like the bear in *The Clever Little Girl and the Bear*. This story comes from Russia. *Foxy-Fox and the Three Bears* is a very old Scottish version of the story which you may know better as *Goldilocks*.

Here are some more stories you might like to read:

About Uninvited Visitors:

The Cock, The Mouse and The Little Red Hen from *The Orchard Book of Nursery Stories* by Sophie Windham (Orchard Books)

About Lucky Escapes:

The Three Little Wolves and the Big Bad Pig by Eugene Trinizas (Egmont Children's Books Limited)

Baba Yaga Bony-legs from *The Orchard Book of Magical Tales* retold by Margaret Mayo (Orchard Books)

Clever Rabbit and King Lion from *The King With Dirty Feet and Other Stories* compiled by Mary Medlicott (Kingfisher)

Class No. _____ J _____ Acc No. _C114477_

Author: _IMPEY ROSE_ Loc: _11 DEC 2001_

LEABHARLANN
CHONDAE AN CHABHAIN

_____

_____

_____

1. **This book may b~ ~pt three weeks. It is to be returned on /~ ~ last date stamped below.**
2. **A fine ~f ~ ~arged for every week or par~ ~rdue.**

C114477
.383